Look and Find®

# HOTEL TRANSYLVANIA 3

*we make books come alive*™

pi kids Phoenix International Publications, Inc.

Chicago · London · New York · Hamburg · Mexico City · Paris · Sydney

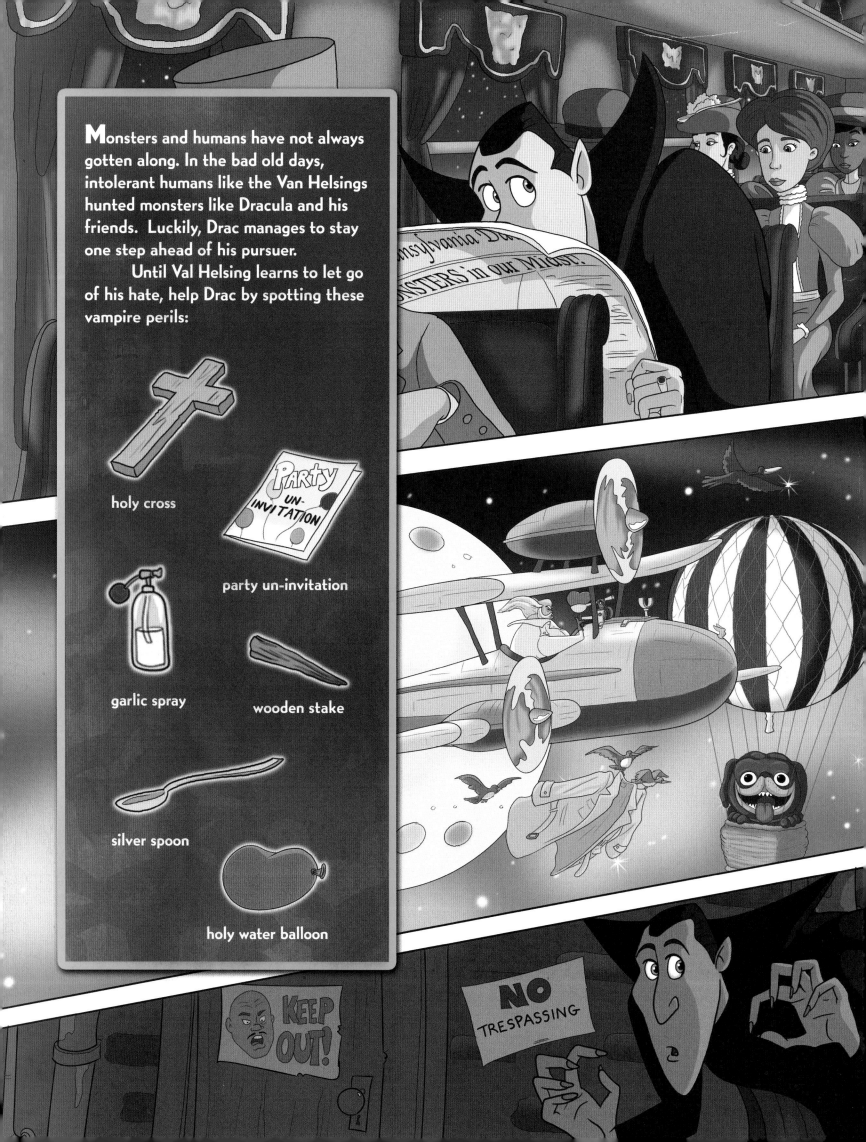

Monsters and humans have not always gotten along. In the bad old days, intolerant humans like the Van Helsings hunted monsters like Dracula and his friends. Luckily, Drac manages to stay one step ahead of his pursuer.

Until Val Helsing learns to let go of his hate, help Drac by spotting these vampire perils:

holy cross

party un-invitation

garlic spray

wooden stake

silver spoon

holy water balloon

Drac built Hotel Transylvania as a vacation spot for monsters tired of dodging humans, and the monsters loved it! People like Van Helsing belong to the past, and humans and monsters get along now, so Drac worries less about safety. Instead, he focuses on more important things...like love!

As Drac and Mavis coordinate the Prickles wedding, mingle with these wedding guests:

Uncle Ned

Bram Shelley Sr. and Jr.

Grandma Lily

Todd

Aunt Agnes

guy no one seems to know

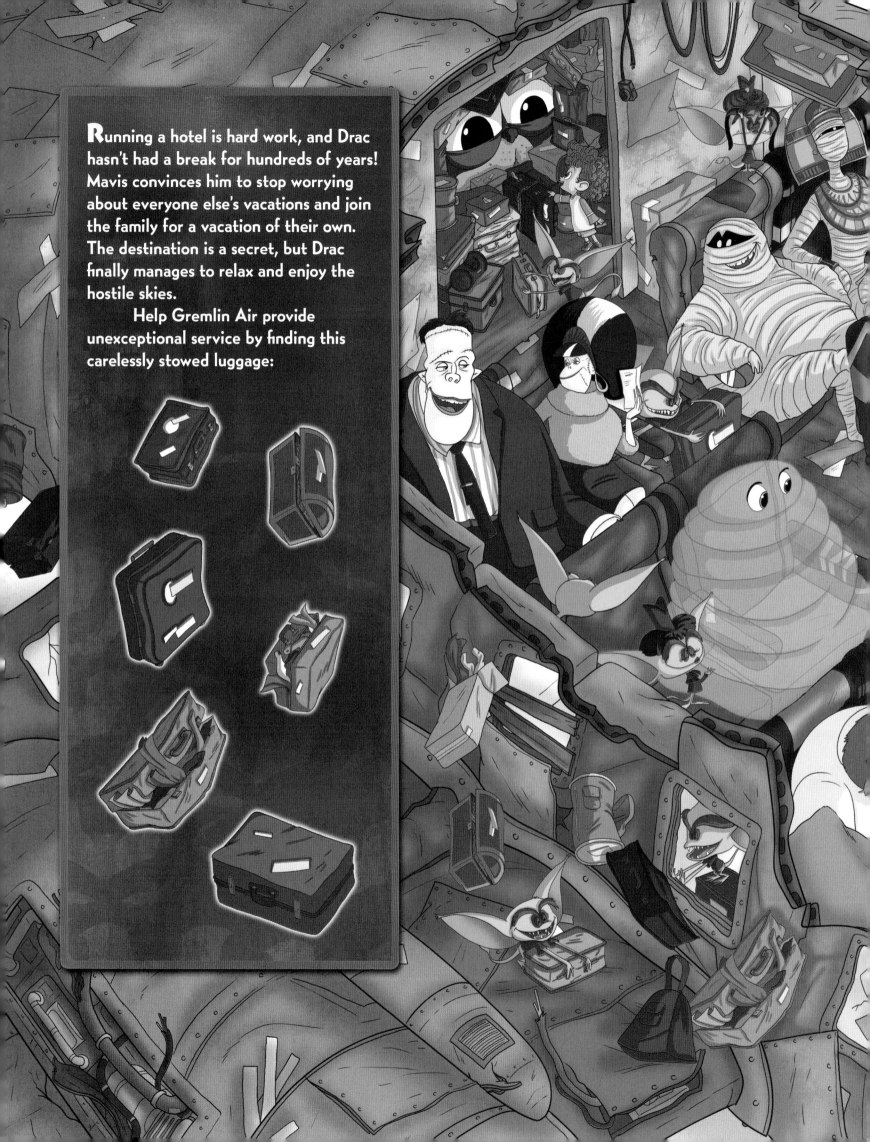

Running a hotel is hard work, and Drac hasn't had a break for hundreds of years! Mavis convinces him to stop worrying about everyone else's vacations and join the family for a vacation of their own. The destination is a secret, but Drac finally manages to relax and enjoy the hostile skies.

Help Gremlin Air provide unexceptional service by finding this carelessly stowed luggage:

After a wonderfully harrowing flight, the Drac-Pack and their families land in the Bermuda Triangle, and Mavis reveals her surprise...a cruise! Drac seems skeptical.

"I'm not getting on some kind of hotel boat," he says, but everyone else is excited to get aboard!

Drac can't see what's so special about a floating hotel. Cast a critical gaze upon these nautical amenities:

Olympic-size waste of space

so-so stairs

mutilating massage

Stan the Fishman

disappointing deck

big whoop buffet

MASSAGE

CRUISE CONSULTANT

visit our OLYMPIC-SIZED POOL

To the MOONBATHING DECK

**W**ayne and Wanda can't believe their eyes when they come across the Kids Club. Why would anyone want to watch their kids for them? On purpose?! But they are not going to stick around questioning it. While the pups play, Wayne and Wanda will do...whatever they want!

Fishman didn't know what he was getting himself into! Help him keep an eye on these wolf pups:

Winston 'n' Wyatt

Watson

Warren wrestling Waylon

Winnie

Wilbur wounding, Wally wincing

Tim

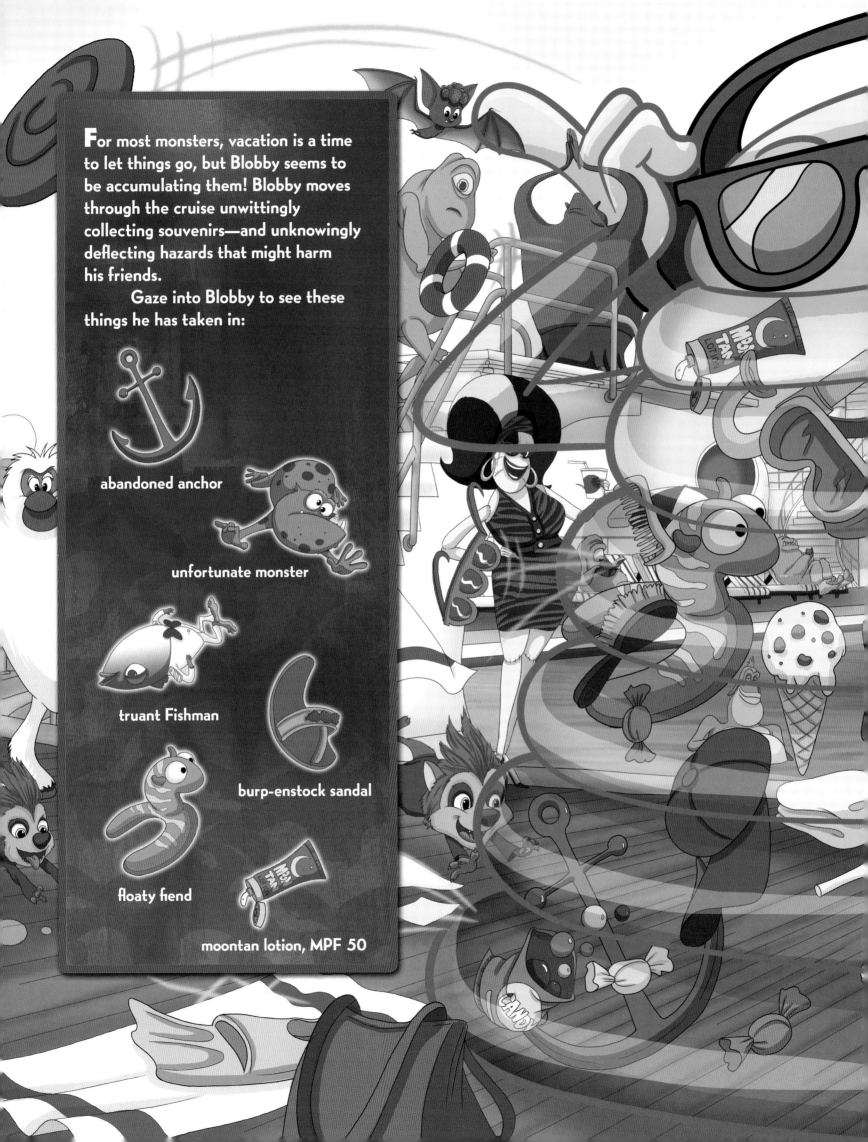

For most monsters, vacation is a time to let things go, but Blobby seems to be accumulating them! Blobby moves through the cruise unwittingly collecting souvenirs—and unknowingly deflecting hazards that might harm his friends.

Gaze into Blobby to see these things he has taken in:

abandoned anchor

unfortunate monster

truant Fishman

burp-enstock sandal

floaty fiend

moontan lotion, MPF 50

The Drac-Pack and their friends love life aboard the cruise ship, but now a new activity beckons—scuba diving! The ship stops above an underwater volcano and everybody slips beneath the ocean surface while the captain keeps a watchful eye.

A world of wonder lies beneath the waves! Keep a lookout for these deep-sea creatures:

manta ray

puffer fish

moray eel

angler fish

lobster

shark

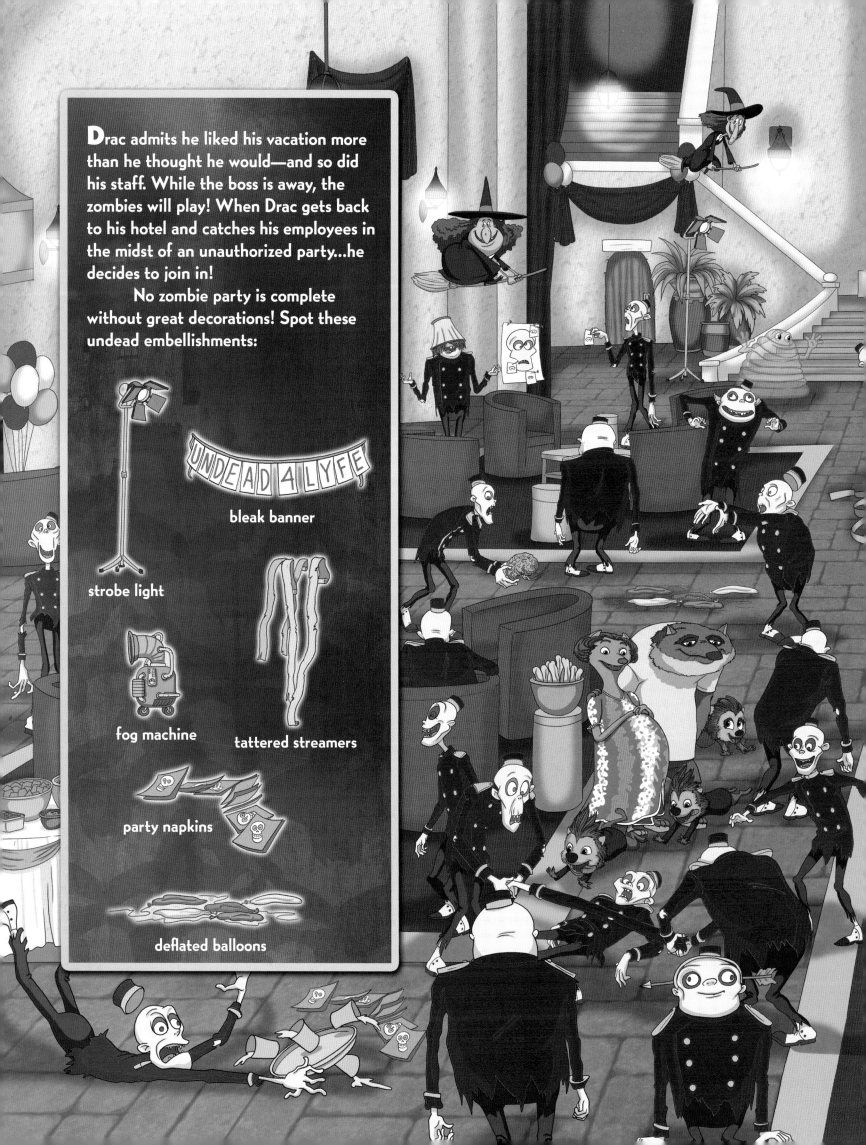

Drac admits he liked his vacation more than he thought he would—and so did his staff. While the boss is away, the zombies will play! When Drac gets back to his hotel and catches his employees in the midst of an unauthorized party...he decides to join in!

No zombie party is complete without great decorations! Spot these undead embellishments:

**strobe light**

**UNDEAD 4 LYFE**
bleak banner

**fog machine**

**tattered streamers**

**party napkins**

**deflated balloons**

Like attitudes, fashions change over time. Revisit earlier eras and find these old-time monster styles:

yeti-felt cloche hat

fear-dora

detachable cape collar

pencil-thin mustache

spider-spun lace gloves

sun-shower resistant trench coat

What's a wedding without finger food? Visit the Prickles' big event again and snack on these horror-d'oeuvres:

rot stickers

devil's eggs

scream cheese on toast

arti*choke* dip

pigs in a casket

eda-mummy

Gremlin Air prides itself on its bottom-notch staff. Board the plane once more and meet this detestable crew:

Cap

Co-Cap

Judy

Junior

Dorothy

Brittni

The cruise draws monsters from all over! Return to the ship and greet these multicultural guests:

gillman from the Black Lagoon

gargoyle from Paris

yeti from Tibet

Baba Yaga from Russia

fly from Canada

Kelsey from Accounting

Help Wayne and Wanda unwind a little longer. Head back to the Kids Club and distract the pups with these monster toys:

Lady Lovibon's anchor

Klabautermann's ladder

dead man's chest

mermaid cave

fly the Dutchman

cannonball pit

"Get jiggly with it!" Bound back and find these items bouncing off of Blobby:

rescue ring

deflected volleyball

missing adventurer's hat

misplaced flipper

three-eyed shades

Baby Blobby

Before wave-ing goodbye, dive deep once more and search for these special seahorses:

The party's not over! Revisit the hotel and join in these undead party games:

piction-scary

brain toss

pin the nose on the zombie's face

three-legged race

limbo

bobbing for Adam's apples

Did you notice an extra monster tucked away on the trip? Dennis managed to sneak Tinkles along for the whole thing! Search every scene for the stealthy stowaway.